Ziji

The Puppy Who Learned to Meditate

Yongey Mingyur Rinpoche
and Torey Hayden

Illustrated by

Charity Larrison

The authors would like to express their gratitude to the many people who have helped bring Ziji to life. They would like especially to thank Anne Benson, Cortland Dahl, Michèle Foetisch, Gerald Godet, and Carole Tonkinson. And an extra special thanks to Michelle La Porte.

About Tergar International

Under the guidance of Yongey Mingyur Rinpoche, the Tergar community of meditation centers and practice groups provides a comprehensive curriculum of meditation training and spiritual study. To learn more about Tergar or to find a program in your area, please contact us.

Tergar International
810 S. 1st St., Suite 200
Minneapolis, MN 55343
Visit our website www.tergar.org
Email us at meditate@tergar.org
Or call us at +1.952.232.0633

Wisdom Publications
199 Elm Street
Somerville, MA 02144 USA
wisdompubs.org

Library of Congress Cataloging-in-Publication Data

Names: Yongey Mingyur, Rinpoche, 1976– author. | Larrison, Charity, illustrator.
Title: Ziji: the puppy who learned to meditate / Yongey Mingyur Rinpoche And Torey Hayden; illustrations by Charity Larrison.
Description: Somerville, MA: Wisdom Publications, 2017.
Identifiers: LCCN 2017005610 (print) | LCCN 2017015729 (ebook)
ISBN 9781614294917 (ebook) | ISBN 9781614294719 (hardcover: alk. paper)
Subjects: LCSH: Meditation—Juvenile literature.
Classification: LCC BL627 (ebook) | LCC BL627 .Y66 2017 (print) | DDC 294.3/4435—dc23
LC record available at https://lccn.loc.gov/2017005610

ISBN 978-1-61429-471-9   ebook ISBN 978-1-61429-491-7

21 20 19 18 17
5 4 3 2 1

Cover and interior design by Annie Hirshman. Set in Marco 15/22.

This is the story of Ziji the dog.

He was about this big:

He had long hair at the top end and shorter hair at the bottom end. It was mostly brown, but some of it was white.

You might think he looked a little bit like a lion. Except for one thing. No lion ever looked as rumpled-up messy as Ziji.

That's because no lion ever loved chasing pigeons as much as Ziji did. Chasing pigeons was Ziji's favorite thing.

Ziji was part of the Anderson family,
along with:

Sometimes the Andersons had fun together.

Sometimes they didn't.

But mostly they were just ordinary.

Maybe a bit like your family.

Ziji and the Andersons lived in an apartment in a tall building.

Across the street was a little park just for the people living in the apartment building to use.

It had a tall fence and a gate to make it very safe.

The Andersons liked going there.

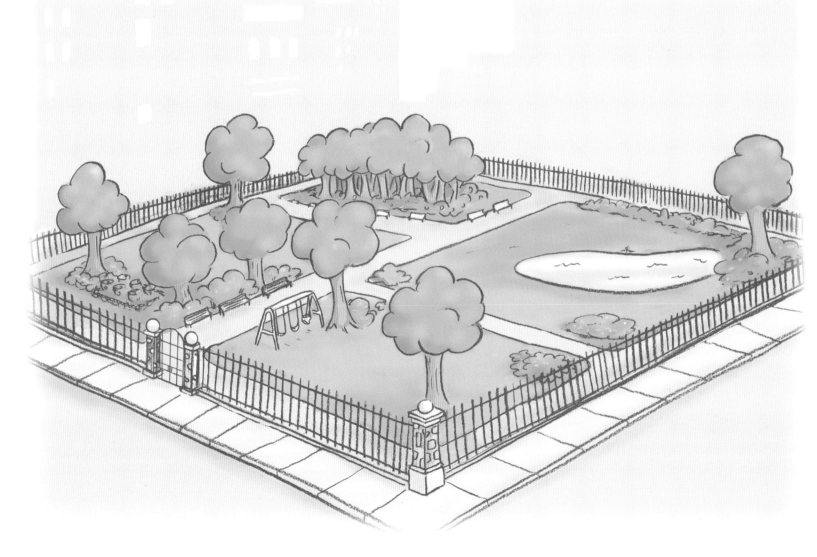

The park was Ziji's most favorite place in the whole world.

Ziji's second most favorite place in the whole world
was on the back of the couch.

From there he could see the park below. It was his park,
so he liked to keep an eye on everything that happened there.

One day Ziji was sitting on the back of the couch, watching his park, when he saw someone new.

A boy about Jenny's age let himself into the park.

Quietly, he walked across the paved area where the pigeons liked to sun themselves.

The pigeons didn't fly up in a whoosh. Ziji started to bark excitedly to tell the boy this was his park.

YAP!
YAP!
YAP!

"What are you barking at?" Jenny asked.
She climbed onto the couch to see out the window.

"That's Nico. His family just moved into the apartment
on the first floor. I saw him at school yesterday. He's in
Mrs. Grayson's class. So you don't have to get so excited.
He's really nice."

Ziji hoped Nico had a ball. Ziji loved playing with balls.
He sat down on the back of the couch to watch.

Nico didn't have anything at all to play with.

Instead, he walked over to the far corner of the park
and sat down on the grass.

Nico sat with his legs crossed and his back straight.
His eyes were almost closed as if he was looking at
something right in front of his nose.

He looked just like the statue by the pond!

The next day Jenny and her friend Sarah
were building a den in the park.
Ziji helped by chasing off the pigeons.

"Ziji, you're being too noisy!" Jenny cried.

YAP!

YAP!

YAP!

Ziji helped in other ways too.

"Ziji, quit stealing our sticks!"

"Ziji, quit bouncing around so much."

Jenny and Sarah didn't want him to play.

Ziji felt bored and left out. He decided
to look for some pigeons to chase.

When Ziji came to the part of the park where the pond was, there was Nico.

The boy was sitting very still, just like he had the day before.

He had a lovely peaceful smile on his face.

Ziji thought, "Here is someone to play with!"
He ran to say hello.

Nico didn't seem to notice him.

Ziji tried his best tricks to get the boy's attention, but they didn't work.

Then Ziji had to be a little more direct.

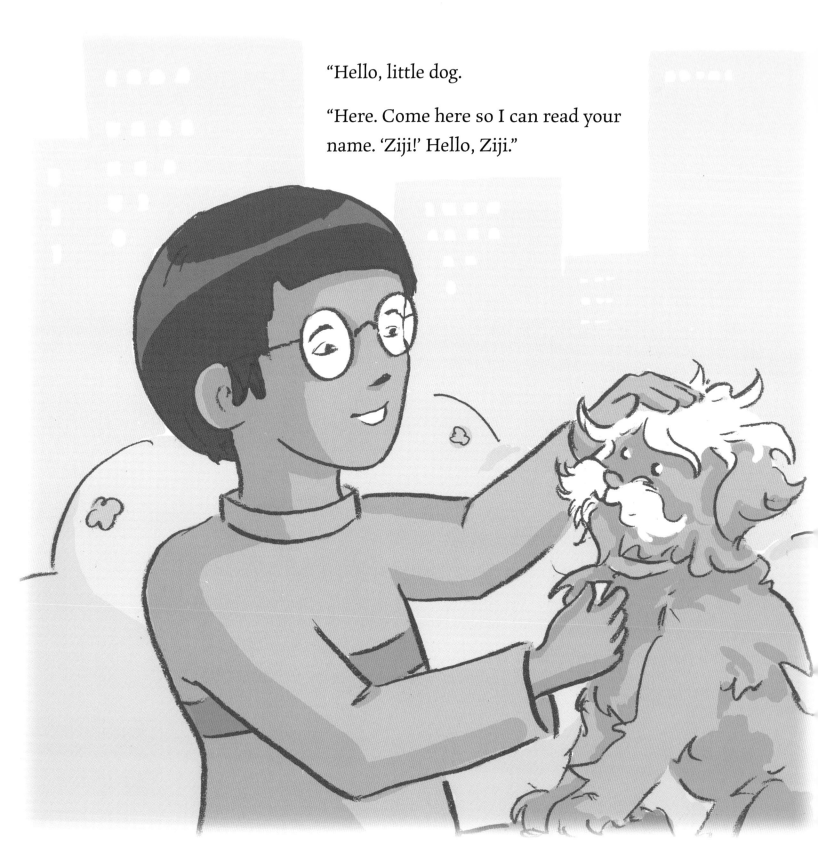

"Hello, little dog.

"Here. Come here so I can read your name. 'Ziji!' Hello, Ziji."

Just then, just beyond where Nico was sitting,
Ziji saw pigeons.

One, two, three, four, FIVE pigeons. In his park!

Ziji would take care of that!!

When he had chased the pigeons off,
Ziji came back.

Perhaps Nico would like to come
with him to look for more pigeons.

That would be fun!

"I understand how exciting it is to make the pigeons fly up, but did you know the pigeons feel very frightened when you do that?" Nico asked in a quiet voice.

"They were enjoying the warm sunshine when suddenly something big and fierce jumped at them and tried to catch them."

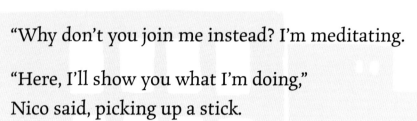

"Why don't you join me instead? I'm meditating.

"Here, I'll show you what I'm doing,"
Nico said, picking up a stick.

"Come over to the pond."

"See what happens in the pond when I whoosh a stick around in it?

"The water gets all muddy because it's been stirred up. Our minds are just like that water and get all stirred up with thoughts and feelings until everything's confused.

"But look. If I stop stirring the water and let it rest, it goes still and then becomes very clear.

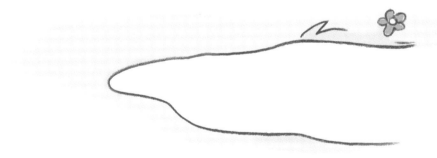

"That's what meditating is. We simply let our mind rest and go still. This way our mind can become clear again, just like the water does."

"I meditate by sitting very quietly like this. I keep my back nice and straight and my muscles relaxed.

"Here, you try it."

"Then I relax my eyes so that they are not looking at anything and feel my breath as it goes in and out. I just barely rest my attention on it."

Just then three pigeons landed right near Ziji.

He forgot all about meditating.

"Yap! Yap! Yap! Yap! Yap!"
Ziji ran this way.

"Yap! Yap! Yap! Yap! Yap!"
Ziji ran that way.

The pigeons flew away frightened.

Nico came over and gently picked Ziji up.

"When something is fun, it is hard to remember others' feelings because we are so busy having a good time.

"But pigeons are just like us.

"They feel unhappy when they are frightened too.

"Here. Let's try again."

"Sometimes things distract us,
but right now we are meditating.

"Instead of following those thoughts
or feelings, we just let them go by.

"We gently bring our attention back
to our breath going in and out."

At home, Ziji went to his favorite place on the back
of the couch to look out the window.

Ziji felt nice and calm inside.

Even though Baby Jack dropped his cookie, Ziji didn't jump down to steal it. He let Baby Jack pick it up again.

The next day when Ziji was crossing the street with Mom and Baby Jack to go to the park, a man on a motorbike came roaring around the corner VERY fast!

"A monster is coming!" Ziji thought. The loud noise and sudden movement gave him a bad fright.

He pulled hard on the leash to get away and it slipped right out of Mom's hand.

Ziji was so scared, he didn't look back. He just ran.

The motorbike-monster came running after him.

"Ziji!" a voice called. It was Nico.
He was on his way to the park too.

When Ziji saw Nico ahead,
he ran toward him.

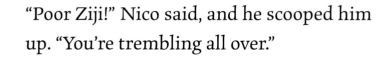

"Poor Ziji!" Nico said, and he scooped him up. "You're trembling all over."

"Oh, thank you so much for catching him!" Mom said to Nico.

"May I help you?" Nico asked.

"I'm going in the park too. Perhaps I can take care of Ziji for you while we're there."

As they came close to the pond,
there was a pigeon having a drink.
"Look out, pigeon!" Ziji barked
enthusiastically. "Here I come!"

"Hold on a minute!" Nico said.

"Remember how you felt when the motorbike came roaring down the street? You were so frightened you ran for your life. That's a horrible feeling.

"When you chase the pigeons, they feel just the same. They think you must be a monster and they feel that horrible scared feeling. It isn't fun to them. Just like being chased by the motorbike wasn't fun for you."

"Come on. Let's give our minds a rest. Let's meditate."

Ziji let his mind go quiet and still. When thoughts came, he let them float by like clouds.

Ziji liked the relaxed, happy way
meditating made his mind feel.

Every day, he practiced a little bit.

Sometimes he practiced
in the park with Nico.

Sometimes he practiced
in the park on his own.

Sometimes he practiced at home.

It wasn't hard at all. When thoughts and feelings came, he just let them float by, while his mind rested.

The Anderson family noticed a change.

"I like how Ziji doesn't bark so much anymore," Mom said. "He seems much happier. And he's more fun to be with when he isn't getting too excited all the time."

"May I join you?" Jenny asked the next day when she saw Ziji running to greet Nico in the park.
"Will you show me what you and Ziji are doing?"

"Yes, of course!" Nico said with a friendly smile.
"It's very easy." Nico picked up a stick.
"Come over to the pond. I'll show you how
our minds can get all stirred up like the water.
And then how we make them nice and clear again!"

On Using This Book—
A Guide for Parents and Teachers

Tibetan meditation master Yongey Mingyur Rinpoche created *Ziji: The Puppy Who Learned to Meditate* in collaboration with child therapist, teacher, and best-selling author Torey Hayden. This book is intended to introduce young children to the practice of meditation.

Almost everyone has heard of meditation, but many of us remain a bit confused about what exactly it is. Scientific research has shown that meditation reduces stress, encourages a longer and healthier life, improves concentration, and promotes a sense of well-being. And it doesn't require expensive equipment or extensive training. It can be done anywhere, by anyone. Yet, for most of us, the word *meditation* conjures up images of austere practitioners of exotic Eastern religions; its relevance to ordinary daily life is not immediately apparent.

Meditation is simply a method to let the mind relax and open. While the mind is usually caught up in the excitement of thoughts and feelings, in meditation we learn to rest it naturally.

Meditation doesn't belong to any particular religion. Though it is often associated with Buddhism, this is simply because Buddhism is a very old religion and its practitioners have been refining the art of meditation for thousands of years. Hindus, Taoists, and followers of other Eastern religions also meditate, but so do Christians, Jews, and Muslims. In these religions it has such names as "contemplative prayer," or it is developed as part of such activities as reflective scriptural reading.

Why has it become a part of so many world religions? Simply because when the mind is quiet, calm, and open, it is more receptive to understanding the essential goodness of the world and the people in it. Yet meditation itself is not a religious practice. It is not tied to any particular religion and will not interfere with anyone's personal beliefs. It is simply a method of cultivating an open, peaceful state of mind.

We live in a very stressful world. The media are constantly priming us with threats of terrorism, violent crime, pandemic disease, economic disaster, and environmental catastrophe, in addition to the personal problems we all experience in our relationships, jobs, health, and finances. Children are particularly susceptible to the ill effects of stress. Unprecedented numbers suffer mental health problems and stress-related illness. Most have lost the carefree lifestyle of the past—leisurely unstructured time at home, the freedom to run and play outside for hours with friends, the security of a close-knit community, and two parents living together in the same house.

Yet the sensitivity of young children is also a great asset. Scientific studies have shown again and again how pliable the brain is at a young age. For this reason, young children can learn to meditate with ease. They are naturally aware and present. Given the right environment, most will take part in meditation enthusiastically.

Meditation can be very helpful for young children.

Not only does it provide them with a ready means of relaxation and a sense of spaciousness amid all the restrictions, pressure, and overstimulation of the modern world, it also helps them understand how their mind works and develop the ability to cope effectively with stressful situations. Preliminary studies suggest that children who learn meditation skills are able to concentrate and think more effectively.

The story of Ziji provides an easy introduction to meditation skills, especially for young children. The following notes are designed to aid adults reading the story to children.

In this story, Ziji learns three things:

1. *What meditation is:* When we meditate, we aren't trying to make our minds do anything unusual or difficult. Instead, we are just resting them. It is normal to have thoughts come into our heads when we meditate. Thinking is what our minds do naturally. But we just let the thoughts go by like clouds in the sky and don't follow them. That's all meditation is.

2. *What happens when we meditate:* Our minds become quiet and calm like a still pond. When we are busy thinking, our feelings and thoughts swirl around, going every which way—sometimes good ways, sometimes not-so-good ways—but always very energetically, the way water does when we vigorously stir it with a stick. And like water that is being stirred, our thinking often gets a bit cloudy due to all these thoughts and feelings spinning around. When we meditate, however, the mind enters a state of rest, becoming clear and calm like a pond left undisturbed.

3. *What happens when the mind is clear and calm:* There are many advantages to the clarity of a relaxed mind. One of them is an increased ability to empathize with others. When we are not caught up in defending "me and mine," we tend to be able to see more clearly how others are just like us. In this are the first seeds of becoming a compassionate person.

At the beginning of the story, we find Ziji living in the midst of the charming but chaotic Anderson family. The Andersons are like most families, but they are also like most of our minds—sometimes fun, sometimes not so fun—we never know what to expect. Ziji, cheerful and bouncy, only thinks about pleasing himself. If he wants a cookie, he steals it from Baby Jack. If he wants excitement, he chases the pigeons. When he meets the boy, Nico, he only sees someone who will play with him. Ziji is like most children!

Thinking Nico is playing a special game and wanting to join in too, Ziji begins to practice meditation. As his ability to meditate improves, he realizes that frantic excitement isn't always pleasant. He begins to feel a sense of inner contentment when he sits quietly with Nico.

When Ziji's mind is full of excitable thoughts and feelings, he is too caught up in them to see how frightened the pigeons are when he chases them. All he thinks of is his own fun. As Ziji learns to meditate, Nico helps him to understand the effects of wild thoughts and feelings. Not only does Ziji begin to feel a sense of inner calm and joy, his quiet mind also lets him become aware of how others—in this case, the pigeons—have feelings just like he does, and that when he chases the pigeons, they feel just as unhappy and frightened as he feels when the motorbike frightens him.

The change isn't just inside Ziji. The Andersons notice how much calmer and happier Ziji seems to be and how much nicer he is to have around. Jenny is curious about what Ziji and Nico are doing together in the park and she decides to join them.

Here are some suggestions for using the book to practice meditation with young children:

1. Point out how rumpled and messy Ziji is at the start of the story. His fur mirrors his "rumpled-up messy" mind. Similarly, we can tell the Anderson family's lifestyle is quite chaotic. There is lots of noise, distraction, and boredom. We see them feeling angry, confused, or overwhelmed. Then talk about Nico. Point out his posture and his nice calm smile and how he is able to help Ziji and the Andersons because he feels calm even when things are chaotic. Show how Ziji looks nice and calm too when he is with Nico. His fur is smoother. He looks happy and rather noble.

2. Explain that meditation helps us learn to be calm and happy like Nico. When we meditate, we aren't trying to make our minds do anything unusual or different. Instead, we are just resting them. Talk about how, when we have been out playing hard and having a good time, we come home and flop down in the chair and go "Ahh," and just rest for a moment. Our bodies are all relaxed and we aren't thinking anything. We are just resting and it feels good. That is all we are doing with our minds during meditation—just letting them rest.

3. Explain that it is normal for a mind to have thoughts. Thinking is what a mind does, just like playing is what a child does. When we are resting our minds, sometimes thoughts turn up, just like when a child is supposed to be resting, but starts to play instead. When that happens, we don't get angry or upset. We just leave the thoughts alone and don't follow them. We let them go by. It's like lying back in the grass and staring up at the sky. Clouds will sometimes float by. We don't chase after them. We just let them float across the sky as we continue to relax in the grass.

4. In the story, Nico helps Ziji deal with the most common problem of meditation—getting distracted by thoughts. Ziji forgets he is meditating and follows his thoughts instead. Nico gently reminds him to bring his attention back to the breath. This allows the distractions or thoughts to "float by like clouds." Help the child understand it is normal to have trouble at first with getting distracted and it isn't something to worry about. Reassure him or her that this is part of learning to do something new and it gets much easier with practice.

5. If children experience frightening or unpleasant thoughts when they are meditating, again, remind them to gently bring their attention back to the breath and as they do that, the "bad" thoughts will vanish.

6. In the story, Ziji uses meditation to develop compassion. He had not realized that from the pigeons' point of view, his chasing them was frightening and upsetting. Nico tells him this, so he hears it intellectually. However, it is when Ziji is sitting quietly and

his mind is very clear that he fully experiences the understanding that he and the pigeons are just alike, that they both experience fear and unhappiness, and in this way he develops compassion toward them.

7. Start with only a minute or two of formal meditation. That is enough for young children. If a child doesn't want to join in, don't force the issue. The most important point is that the child should want to meditate. If it becomes a chore, it won't stick.

8. Most children really enjoy meditation. Often when you introduce them to it, they will pester you to try it again. Children are natural meditators and usually enjoy this new skill, but like all things, it is helpful to do it regularly. Practice makes it much easier to do. If, on the other hand, your children don't seem interested in meditating, then simply read them the book and enjoy the story. A day may come when they ask you to meditate with them.

9. Nico and Ziji are shown doing "formal meditation"—in other words, sitting in a traditional meditation posture. Most children enjoy this posture, but it isn't necessary. Meditation can be done in all sorts of situations and positions. All that is important is that the spine is kept straight. This helps us stay alert and aware. The other thing that makes it "formal" is that Nico has set aside a special time and place to meditate (in this case, in the park by the pond). Having a special time and place to meditate is helpful because it is naturally easier to rest our minds when it is quiet and we are expecting it, just as it is easier to rest our bodies when it is quiet

and we are expecting it. This helps establish a good habit.

10. However, meditation doesn't happen only when sitting in a formal pose and "intending to meditate." It is a natural behavior and can be done anywhere at any time. Encourage children to practice awareness in many situations. Simply stop for a moment and help them to notice what can be seen or heard in the environment, for example, or be aware of the feelings and sensations that are going on inside the body and mind. This is an ideal activity for those many "waiting" moments in the day, such as being stuck in traffic or waiting in a check-out line. These "mini-meditations" lay the groundwork for mindfulness—being aware of what we are doing/thinking/feeling as we are doing/thinking/feeling it. This helps bridge the distance between formal, focused meditation sessions and everyday life.

About the Authors

Born in the Himalayan border regions between Tibet and Nepal, **Yongey Mingyur Rinpoche** is a rising star among the new generation of Tibetan Buddhist masters. His candid, often humorous accounts of his own personal difficulties have endeared him to audiences around the world. His bestselling book, *The Joy of Living: Unlocking the Secret and Science of Happiness*, debuted on the *New York Times* bestseller list and has been translated into over twenty languages. Rinpoche's most recent book is *Joyful Wisdom: Embracing Change and Finding Freedom*.

Born in Montana, **Torey Hayden** has spent most of her adult life working with children in distress. Now living in Great Britain, she provides counseling and advice services for several child-oriented charities. Torey is the author of numerous internationally bestselling books about her experiences as a special-education teacher and a therapist, such as *One Child*, *Ghost Girl*, and *Just Another Kid*. She also has written three novels and *The Very Worst Thing*, a story for eight- to twelve-year-olds. Find her at **www.torey-hayden.com**.